THE AMAZING MARK

Written by Robyn Supraner
Illustrated by Pam Levy

Troll Associates

Library of Congress Cataloging in Publication Data

Supraner, Robyn.
   The amazing Mark.

   Summary: Third-grader Mark describes his school,
home, pets, friends and activities.
   I. Levy, Pam, ill.   II. Title.
PZ7.S9652Am   1986   [E]   85-14070
ISBN 0-8167-0644-1 (lib. bdg.)
ISBN 0-8167-0645-X (pbk.)

10   9   8   7   6   5   4   3   2   1

THE AMAZING MARK

Hi. My name is Mark. I am in
the third grade.

This is Marilyn. She sits next to me. When I put spiders on her desk, she screams. She likes to get me in trouble.

This is Mrs. Hoffman, my teacher. She is going to change my seat if Marilyn doesn't stop screaming.

Mrs. Hoffman believes in the honor system. That means no fighting, no horsing around, and no jumping off desks when the teacher is out of the room. She trusts us.

Mrs. Hoffman has brown hair.
She has blue eyes, the same as
my mother's.

This is my mother. Those are her blue eyes. That is her bicycle.

She likes me to be neat and
clean.

This is how I look when I go to school.

This is how I look when I get home. My mother doesn't understand it. She never will.

She always says:
"I don't understand it. I never
will."

This is Bark, my dog. Mark and
Bark. Bark and Mark. I like the
way it sounds.

14

Bark doesn't go to school, but he is very, very smart.

Bark can play dead. He can roll over and hum. He could sing if he wanted to, but he doesn't know the words.

I am teaching Bark to speak. So
far, he can answer this question:
What is the opposite of smooth?
(Rough!) Pretty smart, don't you
think?

Bark can say his name. He can
say mine, too. It all sounds the
same to my mother, but not to
me. I can tell the difference
because my ear is trained.

This is my room. I made the
sign myself. KEEP OUT AND
THAT MEANS YOU! I made it
for my sister. When you meet
her, you'll know why.

See here? And here? That's how
I keep my room neat and clean.
My mother must have X-ray
eyes.

She always finds out.
"That's not neat and clean," she
says.

The bad thing about my mother is she enters my room without permission. She throws away important things. She says seven toads, four fireflies, two salamanders, and a baby caterpillar may be important to me, but they give her a headache.

My mother gets a lot of
headaches.

The good thing about my
mother is she is the only mom
on the block who can ride a
skate board. I have to give her
credit.

This is Sally. If you are afraid of
snakes, don't look. Sally doesn't
bite. She doesn't sting or do
mean things. Still, some people
hate her. Not me. I even kiss her
—on the lips. Then my mother
turns green.

Say hello to my plant. His name
is Philodendron, but I just call
him Fred.

26

Fred needs water every day.
Sometimes I give him soda. He
likes black cherry best.

Watch out! Here comes Barbara, my little sister. She'll be three in April. She has teeth and everything. You wouldn't believe how strong she is.

My mother calls her Barbie. My
father calls her Boo. Bark calls
her Woof. I like that name best.

My father says Woof is a silly
name for a person. I say it's not
so silly. It's not as silly as Boo.

Woof breaks things. Breaking
things is what she does best.

The thing she loves to say is
"No! No! No! No!"
She does that second best.
She doesn't know as many words
as I do. I give her English
lessons every day.

Woof and Bark do not get along. It is not Bark's fault. He has lots of patience, but Woof uses it up.

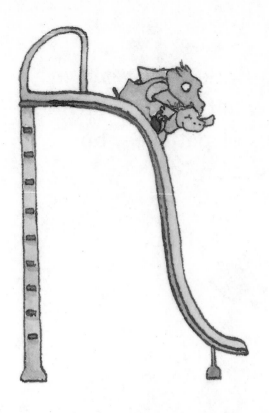

We do things together, Woof
and I—like roll a ball or go on
the slide. Sometimes we get
dressed up. She likes it when I
tickle her. I tickle very gently.

34

Woof isn't so bad. Most of the time she's good. Sometimes I let her kiss me if she's not too sticky.

Bark may not kiss Woof because
of spit and germs. If he has
germs, I never saw them. He
never gave a single germ to me.

That person, the one who is
waving, is Harry. Harry is my
best friend. He's wearing
pajamas because he's sick. Harry
has the mumps. He had them
yesterday, too. He shouldn't be
out of bed. If his mother catches
him . . .

"See you tomorrow, Harry!"

Harry is the president of our
club. I am the vice president.
That means when Harry is in his
room being punished, I am in
command.

The other members of our club
are Robbie, Chuck, and Leo.
We meet three times a week and
decide what to do.

We do things like sell lemonade, or have a circus and sell tickets. Sometimes we go on hikes. We goof around a lot, too.

Do you smell something? It's pot
roast and noodles. My favorite!
Apple pie is for dessert, with
two kinds of ice cream.

I picked the marshmallow-
fudge-ripple. Woof picked
vanilla. She says *banilla*. I am
teaching her to say coconut-
raspberry-swirl.

Well, now you have met
everyone—except my father.
He goes to work in the morning.
At six o'clock he comes home.

My father tells a lot of jokes.
Some of them are funny. His
favorite color is blue, and he
never calls me a baby if I cry.

I hear his key in the door right now!

Sometimes he brings a surprise
for me. He brings surprises for
Woof, too. See! What did I tell
you?

I have to eat my supper now.
Come back again tomorrow. I'll
show you my catcher's mitt.